Peter Rabbit™

PETER'S SECRET MISSION!

D0336187

PUFFIN

Map of my woods

This is a map of the woods where I live. You can see who else lives here too. It's in my dad's journal which I always have with me.

ROCKY ISLAND

Old Brown is very bad tempered. We stay away from him.

OLD BROWN'S ISLAND

MR JEREMY FISHER'S POND

SQUIRREL NUTKIN'S WOOD

MRS TIGGY-WINKLE'S LAUNDRY

Squirrel Nutkin is always getting into some kind of mischief.

Squirrel Tribe Nutkin's cheeky band of squirrel friends.

JEMIMA PUDDLE-DUCK'S
HILLTOP FARM

MR MCGREGOR'S
GARDEN

MR TOD & TOMMY
BROCK'S WOOD

MY BURROW

TUNNEL
NETWORK

DR & MRS BOBTAIL'S
BURROW

MR BOUNCER'S BURROW
(BENJAMIN'S HOME)

RAVINE

DEEP DARK WOODS

DANDELION FIELD

My friend,
Lily Bobtail.
Whatever the
problem, she's
got the answer.

Benjamin Bunny
is my cousin.
Wherever I go,
he's right behind
me – usually hiding!

One breezy autumn morning, Lily and Benjamin arrived at the treehouse to find Peter searching for something.

"What are you looking for?"
asked Lily.

"I can't find my dad's journal,"
Peter replied.

"We'll help you look," said Lily. "Six eyes are better than two – I know that for a fact."

"Someone's taken it," said Peter, "and I think I know who.

We need to go on a secret mission . . ."

The rabbits raced towards the lake. They had to get to Old Brown's island.

"What makes you think that grumpy owl took your dad's journal?" asked Benjamin.

"Old Brown's mad about books," Peter replied.

"It MUST have been him."

At the water's edge, Peter screeched to a stop.

"Look!" Lily pointed. "We can borrow a raft from the squirrels."

"Good idea, Lily!" Peter said as they paddled. "This is better than swimming."

The squirrels were going to Old Brown's island to collect hazelnuts. Lily spotted Squirrel Nutkin on one of the rafts.

"Hi, Nutkin!" she called.

"You can't see me,"
Nutkin called back, hiding behind a leaf.

"I think I know who he's hiding from,"
said Benjamin nervously as they arrived at the island.

Old Brown was snoring loudly up in his tree as the squirrels scampered off to collect nuts.

"He DOES have the journal!" Lily cried, spotting it under the snoozing bird. "But how can we get up there?"

"We need help," Peter said. "Nutkin!"

"Old Brown has taken my
dad's journal," Peter explained.
"We're on a TOP SECRET
mission to get it back.
Will you climb up to get it?"

Nutkin was outraged.
"That nasty old owl!"
he replied. "Of course I will!"

Nutkin clambered up the tree
and stopped right under
Old Brown's razor-sharp talons.
The owl stirred slightly but
then carried on snoring.

Slowly, Nutkin reached for
the journal . . .

"Has he got it?" Benjamin asked, clutching Lily tightly. "Tell me when it's over."

"He's GOT it!" Peter whispered.

"Now, if he can just keep . . ."

"... quiet," Peter finished
as Nutkin shouted,

"WOO-HOO!
I'VE GOT IT!"

Old Brown stirred and opened one eye.

"Got you!" squawked Old Brown, grabbing Nutkin.

Peter gasped.

"We have to rescue him!"

"I've got an idea!" cried Lily.
"Climb on, Peter."

Peter hopped onto the branch of a sapling.
Benjamin and Lily pulled it back hard,
then let go . . .

TWANG!

"Simple but effective,"
Lily said as Peter landed outside Old Brown's treetop house.

"Let him go!"

Peter told Old Brown. "And give me back my dad's journal."

Old Brown just laughed. "You can save your friend. OR you can have the book. It's your choice."

Peter didn't even stop to think. Though the journal was his most precious possession, nothing was more important to him than his friends.

Peter grabbed Nutkin by the hand and,
before Old Brown could change his mind,
the two leaped out of the tree . . .

Luckily, they landed on something soft.
Unluckily, it was Benjamin!

"Ouch. Ouchie. Ow!" Benjamin groaned
as Nutkin scampered off.

"Looks like the journal
is lost forever,"

Peter said sadly.

As the rabbits hopped onto the raft to head home, they heard a frantic scurrying behind them and Nutkin jumped aboard.

"My journal!" exclaimed Peter. "How did you get it without Old Brown noticing?"

"Err, I think Old Brown
DID notice," Benjamin said,
pointing to a dark shape racing
towards them.

"Give me back that book!"
screeched the furious owl.

Old Brown swooped down
towards Nutkin, his sharp
talons gleaming.

Terrified Nutkin cowered behind Peter.
"You can't see me!" he squealed.

"Get away from him!"
Peter shouted.

Picking up one of the hazelnuts the
squirrels had gathered, Peter grabbed
the journal and swung it like a bat . . .

DONK!

The nut hit Old Brown
right between the eyes.

"Tail feathers!"

squawked the beaten bird, before flapping
off back to his island, grumpier than ever.

"Thank you for going back to get my dad's journal," Peter said to Nutkin, when they were safely back in the treehouse.

"Thank you for saving me from Old Brown!" Nutkin replied.

"From now on," Peter said, "I'm going to hide the journal under my bed, where Old Brown will NEVER find it."

"Great idea, Peter," Benjamin said. "And if he comes back, I'll hide under there too!"

A SQUIRREL RAFT

The squirrels are experts at building rafts. They use them on their dangerous nut-collecting missions to Old Brown's island.

Lifeboat (lost!)

Lifebelt

Super-strong string keeps it all together*

*Squirrel knots are TOP SECRET – only squirrels know how to tie them

Flag
(Nutkin "borrowed" it from
Mrs Tiggy-winkle's Laundry)

Squirrel slingshot

Poop deck

Hazelnut heap

Emergency exit
(squirrel overboard!)

Paddle power –
speed 5 nutty knots

Now You SEE Me - Now You DON'T!

Nutkin hid behind a leaf so Old Brown wouldn't see him.

It wasn't a very good hiding place, but don't tell Nutkin!

Play hide-and-seek with your friends and see if you can find some super hiding spots.

YOU COULD TRY HIDING:

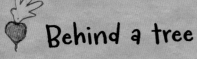 Behind a tree

Under a blanket

In some tall grass

See how long it takes for them to spot you!

CONGRATULATIONS!

SKILL-IN-HIDING CERTIFICATE

Awarded to

Age

Squirrel Nutkin

SQUIRREL NUTKIN
BEST HIDE-AND-SEEKER IN THE WOOD

Hey! You found some
brilliant hiding places!